Yasmin's Parcels

Yasmin's Parcels

by Jill Atkins
and Lauren Tobia

First published 2008
Evans Brothers Limited
2A Portman Mansions
Chiltern St
London W1U 6NR

British Library Cataloguing in Publication Data
Atkins, Jill
  Yasmin's parcels. - (Skylarks)
  1. Children's stories
  I. Title
  823.9'2[J]

ISBN-13: 978 0 237 53585 8 (HB)
ISBN-13: 978 0 237 53597 1 (PB)

Printed in China by WKT Co. Ltd

Series Editor: Louise John
Design: Robert Walster
Production: Jenny Mulvanny

Contents

Chapter One

Yasmin nibbled at the piece of bread in her hand. She was eating slowly, trying to make it last. She knew there was no more food in the house. She looked at the rest of her family. They were all so pale and thin. Mama and Papa and six little brothers and sisters were all squashed into the two dark rooms of their home. Papa was lying on the bed. Mama was rocking the baby in her arms.

"If only Papa's back would get better," sighed Mama. "Then he could find a job."

"And we wouldn't all be so hungry," said Yasmin.

She finished her bread.

"I wonder how your Grandmama is," said Mama.

"I think I'll go round and see her," said Yasmin.

It was very hot outside, but Yasmin hurried along the dusty streets. Soon she reached the tiny old cottage and pushed open the door.

"Hello, Grandmama," she called.

"How are you today?"

"Very well, thank you."

Grandmama's voice sounded croaky
and weak and Yasmin noticed how old
and ill she looked. Grandmama was
hungry, too.

I wish I had something to give her,
thought Yasmin.

After a little while, Yasmin went home. She sat in the corner, thinking. What could she do to help? Suddenly, she had an idea.

"I'm the oldest child in the family," she said to herself. "My family is starving. I must go and find some food."

She jumped up and ran to the door.

"I'm going out," she said.

"Don't be long," said Papa.

"No, Papa."

"Keep away from strangers," said Mama.

"Yes, Mama," called Yasmin as she went out into the street.

Yasmin walked into the town. First, she searched through rubbish bins, but she found nothing to eat there. So she went to the market place. She let her

fingers trail through the beautiful
fluttery silk scarves that rich people
bought. She saw pottery jugs, colourful
clothes, reed baskets, leather sandals
and woven cloths, but she didn't find
any food.

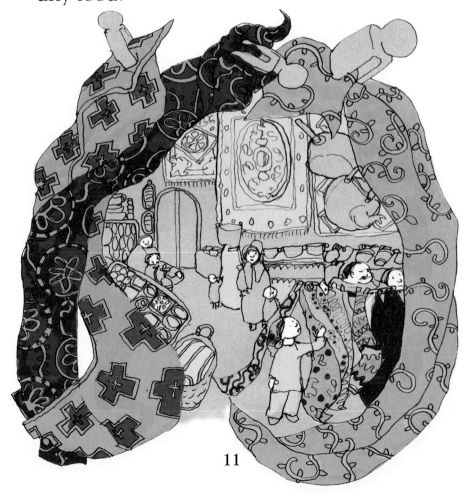

Suddenly, she stopped. There in front of her was a small door that she had never noticed before. The door was ajar so she peeped inside.

"Come in," called an old crackly voice. It made Yasmin jump. She remembered what Mama had told her and she stepped back.

"Who are you?" she called.

Chapter Two

Yasmin heard slow shuffling feet, then the door opened wide. An old man stood in the doorway.

"I'm just an old man who makes pottery jugs," he said to Yasmin. "What do you want?"

"My family is very poor," said Yasmin.

"I'm looking for some food."

"I haven't enough for myself," said the old man, sadly. "I can't help you, but I would be very grateful if you would do something for me."

Yasmin looked at the old man. She couldn't help feeling sorry for him.

"What do you want me to do?" she asked with a smile.

"My kiln has gone out," said the old man. "So I can't fire my beautiful jugs. Will you find me some wood so I can light it again?"

Yasmin was glad to help the old man. She ran along the road and gathered some sticks from under the trees. When her arms were full she carried them back to him.

"Thank you, my friend," said the old man. "You're very kind. I must reward you for your kindness."

He shuffled back inside. Yasmin was
worried. Should she wait for the old
man's reward? He was a stranger. Could
she trust him? She was just about to
walk away when he shuffled back. He
had a parcel in his arms. He gave it to
Yasmin. It was lumpy and quite heavy.

"Don't open it until you really need to," he said.

Yasmin ran home and hid the parcel under her bed. Then she saw that the cupboard was still empty. Everyone was so hungry.

I need to open the parcel now, thought Yasmin. It could be food after all.

She pulled out the parcel and opened it. Inside was an elegant blue and white jug. She put the jug on the table.

"Oh!" she gasped. "Hey! Mama! Look at this!"

The jug was full of milk.

"Where did you get this?" asked Mama.

"An old man gave it to me," said Yasmin, "because I helped him."

Yasmin shared out the milk and put the jug down on the table. Then she picked up her cup and sipped. It tasted so good! She drank it all down in one go and licked her lips. She felt so much better already.

But what a surprise! The jug was full again.

"It's magic," she whispered as she poured some more. Each time she put the empty jug on the table it filled up.

"It's never going to run out," said Yasmin. "I'll take some to Grandmama in the morning."

But in the middle of the night, Yasmin was woken by a sound. Smash! She leapt out of bed just as a cat disappeared out of the kitchen window.

"Oh, no!" Yasmin cried. The jug lay on the stone floor, broken into a thousand pieces.

Chapter Three

Tears trickled down her face as she swept up the pieces.

"What happened?" asked Mama.

"A cat must have knocked it down," cried Yasmin. "And now there's nothing left for Grandmama."

Sadly, Yasmin went back to bed.

In the morning, she looked at her family. Their eyes seemed so big in their thin faces.

"Everyone is still hungry," Yasmin sighed. "I'll have to search for food again." She jumped up and ran to the door.

"I'm going out," she said.

"Don't be long," said Papa.

"No, Papa."

"Keep away from strangers," said Mama.

"Yes, Mama," called Yasmin as she went out into the street.

This time, Yasmin ran along by the river. She searched in the reeds and the mud of the riverbank, but there was no food to be found. She was slowly making her way home when she met an old woman, sitting on the ground with a reed basket in her hands.

"What are you doing?" Yasmin asked.

"Making baskets," said the old woman. "What do you want?"

"My family is starving," said Yasmin. "Have you got any food you could spare us?"

"I have hardly enough for myself," said the old woman. "I can't help you, but perhaps you could do something for me?"

The old woman looked very sad. She reminded Yasmin of Grandmama.

"What would you like me to do?" she asked with a smile.

"I have run out of reeds," said the old woman. "I can't finish making my baskets. Will you find some reeds for me?"

Yasmin ran back along by the river. She collected some reeds and carried them to the old woman.

"Thank you, my friend," said the old woman. "You're very kind. I must reward you for your kindness."

She reached behind her and pulled out a parcel. She handed it to Yasmin.

"Don't open it until you really need to," said the old woman.

Yasmin ran home and hid the parcel under her bed, but it was no good. Everyone was starving.

She fetched the parcel and opened it. Inside was a strong reed basket. Yasmin put it on the table.

"Oh!" she gasped. "Mama! Quick!"
The basket was full of bread.
"Where did you get this?" asked Mama.
"An old woman gave it to me," said
Yasmin, "because I helped her."
Everyone took a piece of bread. It was
the best bread Yasmin had ever tasted.

Her brothers and sisters were smiling. They loved it, too.

Yasmin looked at the basket on the table. But what a surprise! It was full again.

"I'll take some to Grandmama in the morning," said Yasmin as she ate her second piece of bread.

But that night, Yasmin woke in time to see someone climbing out of the window. She saw that the basket had gone.

"Thief!" she cried. "Mama! Papa! The basket has been stolen! Now there's nothing left for Grandmama."

Chapter Four

In the morning, Yasmin's little brothers
and sisters were crying. They were still
hungry. Yasmin knew she had to go
out again.

"They need my help," she sighed.

She jumped up and ran to the door.

"I'm going out," she said.

"Don't be long," said Papa.

"No, Papa."

"Keep away from strangers," said Mama.

"Yes, Mama," called Yasmin as she went out into the street.

Yasmin jogged through the fields to the edge of the mountains.

But the fields were dry and dusty and
the mountains were hard and rocky. She
soon realised she would not find
anything to eat there.

She was just about to return home
and was walking past a big cave in the
side of a mountain when she heard

someone crying. She looked into the cave and saw a boy sitting by a big loom. He looked just like her brother.

"Why are you crying?" she asked.

"I must finish weaving this tablecloth," said the boy. "Or I will be in big trouble."

"So why don't you just finish it?" asked Yasmin.

"I've run out of thread," said the boy and he began to cry again.

"Don't cry," said Yasmin kindly. "I'll see if I can find you some more thread."

She dashed out of the cave and back across the fields. Soon she found some animal hair caught on a bush. She gathered handfuls of the hair and hurried back to the boy.

"But I can't weave that!" cried the

boy. "I need a long thread."

There was a spinning wheel in the corner.

"I'll spin it for you," said Yasmin.

When she had spun the thread, she gave it to the boy.

"But I can't use that!" cried the boy. "It's the wrong colour."

Yasmin sighed, but she ran out into the fields again. She found some berries and carried them back to the cave. She squashed the berries and dyed the thread with the juice. When the boy saw the bright thread, he smiled.

"Thank you, my friend," he said. "You've saved me from an angry master. I must reward you for your kindness."

He reached under the loom and picked up a parcel. He gave it to Yasmin. It was square and very light.

"Don't open this until you really need to," he said.

"Thank you," said Yasmin and she ran home, but she didn't hide the parcel this time.

Chapter Five

Yasmin opened the parcel. Inside was a tablecloth just like the one the boy had been making. She spread it over the table. Suddenly, the table was covered with fantastic things to eat. She stared at the meatballs and rice, the stuffed vine leaves and the peppers, the water

melon and peaches, the apricots
and cherries.

"Come and look at this!" she called.

Mama and all her little brothers and sisters ran to the table. Even Papa got up and stared.

"Where did you get this tablecloth?" Mama asked.

"A little boy gave it to me," said Yasmin, "because I helped him."

40

"You're such a kind girl," said Mama, giving Yasmin a hug. "Thank you."

"Can we eat? Can we eat?" chanted the little brothers and sisters.

Yasmin held up her hand.

"Not yet," she said. "Wait. We can't eat a mouthful until our guest arrives."

41

She left the house and dashed to Grandmama's cottage.

"Quick, Grandmama," she said. "Come with me. I have a surprise!"

Everything was delicious! Mama, Papa, Yasmin, Grandmama and all the little brothers and sisters ate and ate.

But what a surprise! As soon as they had eaten the last mouthful, the table was full again.

That night Yasmin hid the tablecloth under her pillow.

"We must look after this tablecloth for ever," she said.

From that day Yasmin's family were never hungry again. And, most important of all, Yasmin always made sure that there was plenty left for Grandmama!

43

If you enjoyed this story, why not read another *Skylarks* book?

Ghost Mouse
by Karen Wallace and Beccy Blake

When the new owners of Honeycomb Cottage move in, the mice that live there are not happy. They like the cottage just as it is and Melanie and Hugo have plans to change everything. But the mice of Honeycomb Cottage are no ordinary mice. They set out to scare Melanie and Hugo away. They *are* ghost mice after all, and isn't that what ghosts do best?

The Black Knight
by Mick Gowar and Graham Howells

One dark night, a mysterious stranger
visits *The Green Man* inn. He tells the
tale of a magnificent treasure, which
was buried nearby in the time of King
Arthur. This treasure is protected by the
Black Knight. The men in the inn want
the treasure but they are all too afraid
to challenge the fearsome knight.
Tom, the innkeeper's nephew, has
other ideas…

Muffin

by Anne Rooney and Sean Julian

One day, Caitlin finds a baby bird sitting in a broken eggshell. She takes the bird home to the lighthouse and decides to call him Muffin. Muffin is very happy being fed tasty slivers of fish and sleeping in the cosy sock Caitlin has given him, but the time comes when every baby bird must learn to look after itself and Caitlin has to set Muffin free…

Tallulah and the Tea Leaves

By Louise John and Vian Oelofsen

It's the school holidays and Tallulah is bored, bored, BORED! That is, until her Great Granny comes to stay. Tallulah doesn't like Great Granny very much. Not very much at all, really. But, when Great Granny reads the tealeaves, things start to change and Tallulah finds herself in one adventure after another. Suddenly she isn't quite so bored anymore…

Skylarks titles include:

Awkward Annie
by Julia Williams and Tim Archbold
HB 9780237533847
PB 9780237534028

The Black Knight
by Mick Gowar and Graham Howells
HB 9780237535803
PB 9780237535926

Sleeping Beauty
by Louise John and Natascia Ugliano
HB 9780237533861
PB 9780237534042

Ghost Mouse
by Karen Wallace and Beccy Blake
HB 9780237535827
PB 9780237535940

Detective Derek
by Karen Wallace and Beccy Blake
HB 9780237533885
PB 9780237534066

Yasmin's Parcels
by Jill Atkins and Lauren Tobia
HB 9780237535858
PB 9780237535971

Hurricane Season
by David Orme and Doreen Lang
HB 9780237533892
PB 9780237534073

Muffin
by Anne Rooney and Sean Julian
HB 9780237535810
PB 9780237535933

Spiggy Red
by Penny Dolan and Cinzia Battistel
HB 9780237533854
PB 9780237534035

Tallulah and the Tea Leaves
by Louise John and Vian Oelofsen
HB 9780237535841
PB 9780237535964

London's Burning
by Pauline Francis and Alessandro Baldanzi
HB 9780237533878
PB 9780237534059

The Big Purple Wonderbook
by Enid Richemont and Karen Waldek
HB 9780237535834
PB 9780237535957